# MARTHA THE MATHEMAGICIAN

## AND THE SECRET CODE

1★14★4   20★8★5   19★5★3★18★5★20   3★15★4★5

By **LOUISE MATTHEWS** and

Illustrated by **JOHANNA AMOS**

Tarquin

# Publisher's Note

We are excited to introduce Martha to the world and look forward to her adventures in the future. You can get her visit to the Medieval Castle now - details below - and there are more coming soon. You can get more information, free downloads and more about how to use Martha to enjoy learning at www.bigstories.com.

Tarquin has hundreds of mathematics resources - books, posters, games and more - for you and your children to enjoy: **www.tarquingroup.com**

Enjoy the stories: let's make mathematics fun for all!

Book ISBN 9781911093145
Ebook ISBN 9781913565480

---

ISBN (book): 978-1-91109-313-8
ISBN (ebook): 978-1-91356-547-3
Design By Karl Hunt
Printed in the UK

Published by Tarquin
Suite 74, 17 Holywell Hill
St Albans AL1 1DT
United Kingdom
info@tarquingroup.com
www.tarquingroup.com

# Dedication

**For my Dad, Barrie.**

You were so proud of everything I achieved and I wish,
with all my heart, that you could have read this.

Love Little Whizz

**For Milo Hyde and Andrew McSweeney**

Far away in the middle of the ocean lies Calculation Island, a place full of charm and mystery where numbers grow on trees and animals have special mathemagical powers.

High on a rock in the middle of the island stands an old crooked house that looks like it might fall down at any moment. In fact, it is only magic that is holding it in place.

Inside the house lives Max, the Mathemagician. You may be wondering what a mathemagician is ... well, it is someone who can do magic and also loves mathematics. Max is an old man, indeed he is so old that nobody really knows his age. He has a long white beard and wears a purple robe with a pointy hat. He lives with his granddaughter Martha and her best friend, Oscar the Owl.

# M

artha is a sensible girl who likes nothing better than solving mathematical problems and Oscar is devoted to her. He is always by her side but he is extremely clumsy and easily excited.

One day, Martha was sat on a three-legged stool in the corner of the kitchen by the open fire doing what she loved best - solving some tricky mathematical puzzles. Oscar was snoozing on the mantlepiece.

8

**M**ax looked over at her proudly, as she was half way to becoming a mathemagician just like him. She already loved mathematics, she just needed to discover she could do magic too.

He reached up to the mantlepiece and took down an old wooden box. He blew off the dust and handed it to Martha.

"I think that you are ready to have this," he said with a tear in his eye.

**M**artha opened the box and peeped inside to find an old calculator.

"This is the magic calculator," said Max. "To make it work, you need to find the 4 digits that make up the secret code. They are hidden somewhere on Calculation Island. Once you find the secret code you will be able to help people with their mathematical problems just like me."

"I don't know where to start looking," said Martha, looking most confused.

"Don't worry about that," said Max. "There are lots of mathemagical creatures on the island who will be able to guide you"

"Oh, I see," replied Martha hesitantly.

"**O**scar will help you too," said Max as he poked the startled owl who was still snoozing on the mantlepiece.

Martha picked up the magic calculator and slid it into the pocket of her pinafore dress and set off with Oscar to find the secret code.

They stepped out of the crooked house into the garden. Oscar ran on ahead. Before too long he tripped and fell head first into the cabbage patch.

"**O**h, Oscar you are clumsy," laughed Martha. "What have you tripped over now?"

"I don't know," replied Oscar. "But I have hurt my beak"

Oscar sat up and rubbed his beak and then they heard the sound of crying coming from the cabbage patch. Out of the leaves appeared a very large ladybird with tears rolling down her face.

"Oh dear," said Martha. "Did my clumsy friend hurt you when he tripped?"

"No, it's not that," replied the ladybird. "I am the halving ladybird. I like to halve things and I am crying because the spots on my back have all gone wrong. I like to have half on one side and half on the other and look what has happened. I feel all lopsided."

### Questions for the reader

How many spots does she have altogether?

How many on this side?

How many on that side?

Does she have half on each side?

How do you know?

What could Martha do to help?

**M**artha and Oscar looked at the ladybird's back where there were 10 spots, 7 on one side and 3 on the other side.

"Don't cry," said Martha, stroking the ladybird's head. "I can help you." She quickly peeled two spots from one side of the ladybird and put them onto the other side. "There," she said that should do it.

"Thank you," said the ladybird. "I feel much better now."

## Questions for the reader

How many spots does she have altogether now?

How many on this side?

How many on that side?

Does she have half on each side? How do you know?

Has Martha solved the problem?

Oscar flapped his wings with glee. "You are clever Martha," he said.

"Before I go," said the halving ladybird. "I have a clue to the secret code. **The first digit is half of 6.**"

"Thank you," said Martha. "That is really helpful. Now we must be on our way as we have three more clues to find."

Martha and Oscar left the garden and wandered through the forest where numbers grow on trees looking around them for the next clue to the secret code.

"There are plenty of numbers growing in the trees," said Martha, "but I just don't know which ones I need for the secret code." It was a warm summer's day so they sat down under a tree to shade from the afternoon sun.

Just then there was a rustling in the trees and along came a jolly looking crocodile.

"Hey look!" said Martha. "Here comes a Crocodile." But Oscar was nowhere to be seen. He was so scared that he had flown up into the tree. When Martha looked up, he was sitting on a branch with his knees knocking together in fright.

"**O**scar come down and meet him. There is no need to be afraid. He is a Number-Eating Crocodile and he only eats numbers."

"He d-d-d-d-doesn't like to e-e-e-e-e eat owls then," said Oscar nervously.

"No, I don't," said the crocodile. "Owls would be disgusting. I only eat numbers and the bigger the better."

Oscar flew down from the tree carrying an 8 and a 3. "I have two numbers here," he said, "and I want to give you the bigger one but they both look the same size to me."

**8   3**

**M**artha smiled at her feathered friend and said "Oscar, that is because when we talk about numbers being bigger or smaller, we are thinking about how many the number represents not the size of the actual number."

She quickly drew two ten-frames on the ground in the mud with a stick and placed some leaves onto them.

## Questions for the reader

How many leaves are in the first ten-frame?

How many leaves are in the other ten-frame?

Which ten-frame has more leaves?

Which ten-frame has fewer leaves?

Which is the bigger number?

Which is the smaller number?

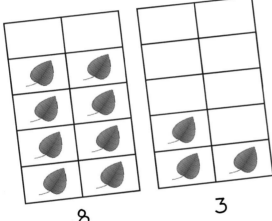

8          3

"**N**umber-Eating Crocodiles always eat the bigger number," said Martha. "We know that 8 is bigger than 3 so he will eat the 8." The crocodile ate the 8 and left the 3 just as Martha had predicted.

"Thank you for the snack," said the Number Eating Crocodile. "Before I go, I have the clue to the second digit of the secret code. **The second digit is bigger than 4 and smaller than 6.**"

"Thank you," said Martha. "That is really helpful. Now we must be on our way as we have two more clues to find."

**M**artha and Oscar continued on their journey. They came out of the woods and found themselves on top of a cliff looking out to sea.

"Wow," said Oscar. "This looks like a wonderful place to fly" as he flapped his wings and took off into the bright blue sky. "Look at me," he said as he began looping round not really watching where he was going.

"Look out!" cried Martha but it was too late he flew straight into a giant butterfly and they both fell to the ground. Oscar landed ungracefully onto the soft grass below and the butterfly landed on top of him.

"I'm Ok," mumbled Oscar poking his head out from beneath the butterfly's wing.

"Well I'm not," said the butterfly angrily. "What did you think you were doing flying around like that? Don't you know how dangerous that is?"

"I'm really sorry," said Oscar. "I was showing off and I didn't see you."

"Here, let me help you," said Martha as she pulled the butterfly to his feet. "Wow, your wings are so beautiful."

The butterfly seemed to forget that he was cross. He was a little vain and enjoyed the compliment. He stretched his wings out fully so they could get a better look. "I am the Doubling Butterfly," he said. "If you give me a number, I can double it for you."

"Ok," said Oscar.

"If you are so clever what is double 3?"

The butterfly stretched out one of his wings and 3 stars appeared it.

"Here is your 3," he said, "and now I am going to double it." He stretched out his other wing and 3 stars appeared on that wing too.

## Questions for the reader

How many stars are on the first wing?

How many stars are on the other wing?

What number are you doubling?

How many stars are there altogether?

So double ..... is .....

"Wow," said Oscar flapping his wings with glee (he does that a lot!) "I can easily see that double 3 is 6. Again, again, what is double 5?"

The butterfly stretched out his wings again, 5 stars appeared on one wing and then 5 stars appeared on the other wing.

## Questions for the reader

How many stars are on the first wing?

How many stars are on the other wing?

What number are you doubling?

How many stars are there altogether?

So double ..... is .....

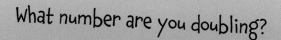

"Wonderful," said Martha. "We can see that double 5 is 10."

"Well seeing as you have been so complimentary about my beautiful wings, I will give you the third clue to the secret code. **The third number is double 4**."

"Thank you so much," said Martha gratefully. "Now we must be on our way as we still have one more clue to find." They waved goodbye to the doubling butterfly as he flew off over the cliff top.

"Come on," said Martha. "Let's go down onto the beach and try to stay out of trouble."

They climbed down the path, stepped onto the sand and began walking along the beach as the sea lapped gently beside them.

"Look what I have found!" cried Oscar. "It is a lovely blue hat." He picked up what he thought was a hat and popped it on his head. "How do I look?" he said doing a silly dance to show off his new headwear.

Suddenly they heard a voice shouting "Hey, what are you doing with my sock?" They both turned around to see a cross looking starfish perched on a rock by a rockpool. He was wearing 2 blue socks and 2 white socks; his other foot was bare.

"I'm sorry," said Oscar. "I thought it was a hat". He removed the sock from his head and handed to back to the starfish who put it on his remaining foot.

33

"No harm done. I am glad that you found it. I have been looking for it for ages," said the starfish.

"But I need 5 socks because I am the Making Five Starfish. Today I am wearing 3 blue socks and 2 white socks! 3 and 2 make 5 see?"

## Questions for the reader

How many white socks is he wearing?

How many blue socks is he wearing?

How many socks does he have altogether?

So ___ and ___ makes 5.

"I am loving your socks," said Martha with a smile. "What sock combination are you going to be wearing tomorrow?"

"**W**ell," replied the starfish. "Tomorrow I am going to be wearing 4 white socks..."

"Ooh ooh," interrupted Oscar in excitement. "I know that means you will be wearing 1 blue sock because 4 white socks and 1 blue sock also makes 5."

"That's right. I have lots of options with my blue and white socks and they are obviously starfish socks and not owl hats," he said while laughing at Oscar.

## Questions for the reader

How many white socks is he wearing?

How many blue socks is he wearing?

How many socks does he have altogether?

So __ and __ makes 5.

How many other ways can he wear his socks?

36

"Anyway. Before you go," said the Starfish.

"As a way of saying thank you for finding my hat...I mean...sock," he stumbled.

"I would like to provide you with the fourth clue to the secret code. The clue is **the number you would add to 3 to make 5**."

"Thank you," said Martha. "That is fantastic. We now have all four clues."

"Come on Oscar. Let's see if we can work it out."

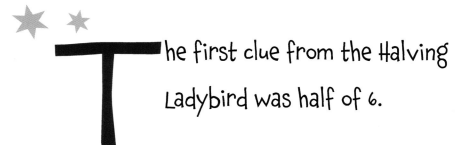

The first clue from the Halving Ladybird was half of 6.

The second clue from the Number Eating Crocodile was bigger than 4 and smaller than 6.

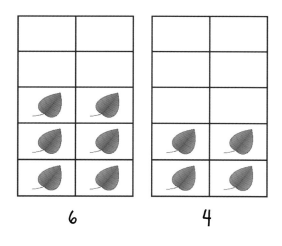

6          4

The third clue from the Doubling Butterfly was double 4.

The fourth clue from the Making Five Starfish was the number you would add to 3 to make 5.

"ave you worked it out?" asked Oscar.

"Yes, I have got it," said Martha.

"The secret code is **3 5 8 2**".

"Well done," said Oscar, flapping his wings with glee (again!)

Martha took the magic calculator from her pinafore
dress pocket and it began to flash.
She keyed in the secret code and
they both disappeared in a puff
of smoke.

They reappeared back in their old house by the fire in the kitchen. Grandad Max beamed with joy. "Well done Martha, you have correctly entered the secret code and the magic calculator is activated. You are now a fully qualified Mathemagician. I am so proud of you.

F rom now on, whenever the magic calculator flashes, it means that somewhere in the world, someone needs your help with a mathematics problem and you will be transported there to give them help. Don't worry as Oscar will always go with you to keep you out of trouble."

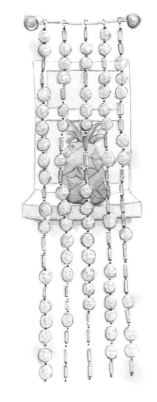

"Mmm," said Martha looking at her feathered friend. "I'm not sure about that!"

# Follow up Activities

- Give the child an even number of small items (buttons, counters, bottle tops etc.) and ask them to find half of them using the Halving Ladybird. When they have finished ask them to describe what they have done in a sentence.

  "Half of... is ..."

- Write down two numbers for the child and ask them to make each number on a different ten ten-frame using small items (buttons, counters, bottle tops etc.) Then ask them to tell you which is the bigger number and which is the smaller number. Encourage them to answer in a full sentence.

  "... is bigger than..."     ". . . is smaller than ..."

- Take it in turns to close your eyes whilst the other player places a number of small items (buttons, counters, bottle tops etc.) on one wing of the Doubling Butterfly. The other player has to say what would happen if they were doubled using a full sentence.

"Double ... is ..."

- Using the Making Five Starfish find all the ways of making five by placing small items of two colours on his feet. Encourage them to speak in full sentences.

"__ and__ make 5"

# The Halving Ladybird

# The Tens Frames

# The Doubling Butterfly